The Noble Quran Folklore

Ababil The Flocks of Birds Army from Heaven English Edition

by

Muhammad Hamzah Sakura Ryuki

2023

Muhammad Hamzah Sakura Ryuki

Publishing

2023

Muhammad Hamzah Sakura Ryuki

Prolog

Allah SWT (God) Said:

{And He sent against them birds, in flocks. Striking them with stones of Sijjil (baked clay). And made them like an empty field of stalks (of which the corn has been eaten up by cattle).}

(The Noble Quran Surah Al-Fil: 3–5)

While meekness is a characteristic of most visual creatures in the universe, then the frightful horror constitutes a characteristic of their unknown counterparts. I will not say anything else ...

I am not allowed to talk about myself.

Chapter 1

My reality encloses a secret which if it is revealed to any creature, his blood will freeze and he will cease to exist out of fright.

I am Ababil one of the "Flocks of Birds from Heaven," that was mentioned in The Noble Qur'an. I am the Commander of Communications among the six wings of the Eighth Army of these birds. The number of armies is a secret as well as the number of birds in the Eighth Army.

We launch wars only at the order of Almighty Allah SWT The Lord of Universe. I will not say how many missions we have carried out, for this matter belongs only to Almighty Allah.

"Every day He has a matter to bring forth (such as giving honor to some, disgrace to some, life to some, death to some, etc.)!"

All what I can say is that those missions were known to the Cherisher and Sustainer of the worlds.

As for us creatures, there are cascading curtains and thick barriers that separate between them and us and this is because of Allah SWT (God) mercy to His servants.

Chapter 2

Allah SWT (God) has mentioned two of these missions in His last Book (The Ever-Glorious Noble Qur'an) to mortals. The first mission was to strike the cities of Prophet Lut AS (Lot).

Almighty Allah SWT says, "So when Our Commandment came, We turned (the towns of Sodom in Palestine) upside down, and rained on them stones of baked clay, piled up. Marked from your Lord, and they are not ever far from the Zalimun (polytheists, evil-doers, etc.)."

During this mission we were not mentioned by name in the context of the verses.

The second mission in which Almighty Allah SWT has mentioned us in by name was the strike on the Owners of the Elephant...

The Exalted says, "Have you (O Muhammad (Peace be upon him)) not seen how your Lord dealt with the Owners of the Elephant?

[The elephant army which came from Yemen under the command of Abrahah Al-Ashram intending to destroy The Holy Ka'bah at Makkah]. Did He not make their plot go astray?

And sent against them birds, in flocks. Striking them with stones of Sijjil (baked clay). And made them like an empty field of stalks (of which the corn has been eaten up by cattle). "

I was the first one to receive the order. I screamed out and so the army gathered around. My scream made the farthest star tremble and its atoms shook out of evil omen, and the blood froze in the mountains' veins and its summits became adorned with deathly white snow.

And a wave of mysterious terror vibrated through the atmosphere of the earth.

Chapter 3

One second after my scream, the whole Eighth Army gathered upon the branches of fear, the trees of terror and the desolateness of destruction and emptiness.

The Commander of the birds asked, "Who has summoned us forth from the depths of Hell?"

I said, "This is Allah SWT The Creator of Earth & Heaven Will."

The birds prostrated in terror …while they themselves are originally the source of absolute terror.

The Commander said, "What is our mission?"

I said, "To strike an army heading towards The Holy Ka`bah with the intention to destroy it."

The birds bowed their beaks and dipped them in Hellfire … they delved into it with their beaks and brought out stones of Sijjil from Jahannam hellfire.

At the same time pictures were taken of the attacking army that helped us make a quick estimation of the forces required to destroy our enemy.

And, each one of the "Flights of Birds" was bestowed with a power enough to destroy Abraha's army. We organized our formations and plans in Hell-fire and headed silently towards the enemy.

Chapter 4

Abraha's army depended mainly on infantry, made up of cavaliers and armors … the elephants were the armors. Abrahas' army lacked an air force. This was where we had the upper hand over his army.

We were on the way to bomb him from the air.

The artillery had not been discovered until at that time …but we knew that the artillery would not affect us. We were on our way to strike him with stones of Sijjil.

In these stones lies an incredible secret. My revealing a part of it will only make its mystery even deeper. It would be centuries after our strike on Abraha that humans would discover the energy latent in the nucleus.

They will invent bombs made of nuclear energy.

These bombs will have a destructive power not present in unpossessed by traditional weapons. This nuclear energy in comparison to the stones of Sijjil is as innocent as children's toys.

This is all I can say concerning the destructive power that was used against Abraha's army. These are the limits that I can reveal. I do not want to elaborate more.

We were tremendous in number when we attacked Abraha's army. I was the first to see the armors of this evil army.

There was a gigantic elephant at the head of the army and behind him were many elephants. I caught a glimpse of his trembling frame despite of my height. I knew that he was trembling because of the vibrations of the air.

Chapter 5

The elephant was sitting, and then he suddenly got up and ran towards the desert in an attempt to save himself. I threw the first stone from Hell amidst the army… Abraha's army blew up.

The explosion was confined to a certain area. The destructive power was not allowed to explode in its natural way in the surrounding areas nor was it allowed to make a loud noise.

The explosion was silent and was confined to the enemy's army. The explosion was controlled, not free. For, if it was allowed free reign, it would have completely destroyed The Holy Ka'bah and all the surrounding areas and it would be impossible to save them after that.

The explosion was silent. Its sound died of fear before it had even been born.

And, the rest of the "Flocks of Birds" dropped the stones that they were carrying in their beaks.

Later, historians will write that Abraha had retreated and his flesh was falling off piece after piece along the way.

However, this description is not accurate, because the truth is that Abraha's army turned into an empty field of stalks of which the corn had been eaten up by cattle.

They turned to be like the dung of animals. And finally the wind swept away what was left of Abraha's army.

Author Biography

We will remove whatever bitterness they had in their hearts. Rivers will flow under their feet.

And they will say, "Praise be to Allah SWT for guiding us to this. We would have never been guided if Allah SWT had not guided us.

The messengers of our Lord had certainly come with the truth." It will be announced to them,

"This is Jannah Paradise awarded to you for what you used to do."

(The Holy Quran Surah Ar-Ra'd verse 23-24)

Muhammad Hamzah Sakura Ryuki

www.ingramcontent.com/pod-product-compliance
Lightning Source LLC
LaVergne TN
LVHW020426070526
838199LV00004B/289